A NEW LEAF

A NEW LEAF

FRANCIS SCOTT FITZGERALD

ISBN: 978-93-5342-059-8

First Published: 1931

LECTOR HOUSE LLP
E-MAIL: lectorpublishing@gmail.com

A NEW LEAF

BY

F. SCOTT FITZGERALD

1931

A NEW LEAF

It was the first day warm enough to eat outdoors in the Bois de Boulogne, while chestnut blossoms slanted down across the tables and dropped impudently into the butter and the wine. Julia Ross ate a few with her bread and listened to the big goldfish rippling in the pool and the sparrows whirring about an abandoned table. You could see everybody again--the waiters with their professional faces, the watchful Frenchwomen all heels and eyes, Phil Hoffman opposite her with his heart balanced on his fork, and the extraordinarily handsome man just coming out on the terrace.

> *--the purple noon's transparent might.*
> *The breath of the moist air is light*
> *Around each unexpanded bud--*

Julia trembled discreetly; she controlled herself; she didn't spring up and call, "Yi-yi-yi-yi! Isn't this grand?" and push the maître d'hôtel into the lily pond. She sat there, a well-behaved woman of twenty-one, and discreetly trembled.

Phil was rising, napkin in hand. "Hi there, Dick!"

"Hi, Phil!"

It was the handsome man; Phil took a few steps forward and they talked apart from the table.

"--seen Carter and Kitty in Spain--"

"--poured on to the Bremen--"

"--so I was going to--"

The man went on, following the head waiter, and Phil sat down.

"Who is that?" she demanded.

"A friend of mine--Dick Ragland."

"He's without doubt the handsomest man I ever saw in my life."

"Yes, he's handsome," he agreed without enthusiasm.

"Handsome! He's an archangel, he's a mountain lion, he's something to eat. Just why didn't you introduce him?"

"Because he's got the worst reputation of any American in Paris."

"Nonsense; he must be maligned. It's all a dirty frame-up--a lot of jealous husbands whose wives got one look at him. Why, that man's never done anything in his life except lead cavalry charges and save children from drowning."

"The fact remains he's not received anywhere--not for one reason but for a thousand."

"What reasons?"

"Everything. Drink, women, jails, scandals, killed somebody with an automobile, lazy, worthless--"

"I don't believe a word of it," said Julia firmly. "I bet he's tremendously attractive. And you spoke to him as if you thought so too."

"Yes," he said reluctantly, "like so many alcholics, he has a certain charm. If he'd only make his messes off by himself somewhere--except right in people's laps. Just when somebody's taken him up and is making a big fuss over him, he pours the soup down his hostess' back, kisses the serving maid and passes out in the dog kennel. But he's done it too often. He's run through about everybody, until there's no one left."

"There's me," said Julia.

There was Julia, who was a little too good for anybody and sometimes regretted that she had been quite so well endowed. Anything added to beauty has to be paid for--that is to say, the qualities that pass as substitutes can be liabilities when added to beauty itself. Julia's brilliant hazel glance was enough, without the questioning light of intelligence that flickered in it; her irrepressible sense of the ridiculous detracted from the gentle relief of her mouth, and the loveliness of her figure might have been more obvious if she had slouched and postured rather than sat and stood very straight, after the discipline of a strict father.

Equally perfect young men had several times appeared bearing gifts, but generally with the air of being already complete, of having no space for development. On the other hand, she found that men of larger scale had sharp corners and edges in youth, and she was a little too young herself to like that. There was, for instance, this scornful young egotist, Phil Hoffman, opposite her, who was obviously going to be a brilliant lawyer and who had practically followed her to Paris. She liked him as well as anyone she knew, but he had at present all the overbearance of the son of a chief of police.

"Tonight I'm going to London, and Wednesday I sail," he said. "And you'll be in Europe all summer, with somebody new chewing on your ear every few weeks."

"When you've been called for a lot of remarks like that you'll begin to edge into the picture," Julia remarked. "Just to square yourself, I want you to introduce that man Ragland."

"My last few hours!" he complained.

"But I've given you three whole days on the chance you'd work out a better approach. Be a little civilized and ask him to have some coffee."

As Mr. Dick Ragland joined them, Julia drew a little breath of pleasure. He was a fine figure of a man, in coloring both tan and blond, with a peculiar luminosity to his face. His voice was quietly intense; it seemed always to tremble a little with a sort of gay despair; the way he looked at Julia made her feel attractive. For half an hour, as their sentences floated pleasantly among the scent of violets and snowdrops, forget-me-nots and pansies, her interest in him grew. She was even glad when Phil said:

"I've just thought about my English visa. I'll have to leave you two incipient love birds together against my better judgment. Will you meet me at the Gare St. Lazare at five and see me off?"

He looked at Julia hoping she'd say, "I'll go along with you now." She knew very well she had no business being alone with this man, but he made her laugh, and she hadn't laughed much lately, so she said: "I'll stay a few minutes; it's so nice and springy here."

When Phil was gone, Dick Ragland suggested a *fine* champagne.

"I hear you have a terrible reputation?" she said impulsively.

"Awful. I'm not even invited out any more. Do you want me to slip on my false mustache?"

"It's so odd," she pursued. "Don't you cut yourself off from all nourishment? Do you know that Phil felt he had to warn me about you before he introduced you? And I might very well have told him not to."

"Why didn't you?"

"I thought you seemed so attractive and it was such a pity."

His face grew bland; Julia saw that the remark had been made so often that it no longer reached him.

"It's none of my business," she said quickly. She did not realize that his being a sort of outcast added to his attraction for her--not the dissipation itself, for never having seen it, it was merely an abstraction--but its result in making him so alone. Something atavistic in her went out to the stranger to the tribe, a being from a world with different habits from hers, who promised the unexpected--promised adventure.

"I'll tell you something else," he said suddenly. "I'm going permanently on the wagon on June fifth, my twenty-eighth birthday. I don't have fun drinking any more. Evidently I'm not one of the few people who can use liquor."

"You sure you can go on the wagon?"

"I always do what I say I'll do. Also I'm going back to New York and go to work."

"I'm really surprised how glad I am." This was rash, but she let it stand.

"Have another *fine*?" Dick suggested. "Then you'll be gladder still."

"Will you go on this way right up to your birthday?"

"Probably. On my birthday I'll be on the Olympic in mid-ocean."

"I'll be on that boat too!" she exclaimed.

"You can watch the quick change; I'll do it for the ship's concert."

The tables were being cleared off. Julia knew she should go now, but she couldn't bear to leave him sitting with that unhappy look under his smile. She felt, maternally, that she ought to say something to help him keep his resolution.

"Tell me why you drink so much. Probably some obscure reason you don't know yourself."

"Oh, I know pretty well how it began."

He told her as another hour waned. He had gone to the war at seventeen and, when he came back, life as a Princeton freshman with a little black cap was somewhat tame. So he went up to Boston Tech and then abroad to the Beaux Arts; it was there that something happened to him.

"About the time I came into some money I found that with a few drinks I got expansive and somehow had the ability to please people, and the idea turned my head. Then I began to take a whole lot of drinks to keep going and have everybody think I was wonderful. Well, I got plastered a lot and quarreled with most of my friends, and then I met a wild bunch and for a while I was expansive with them. But I was inclined to get superior and suddenly think 'What am I doing with this bunch?' They didn't like that much. And when a taxi that I was in killed a man, I was sued. It was just a graft, but it got in the papers, and after I was released the impression remained that I'd killed him. So all I've got to show for the last five years is a reputation that makes mothers rush their daughters away if I'm at the same hotel."

An impatient waiter was hovering near and she looked at her watch.

"Gosh, we're to see Phil off at five. We've been here all the afternoon."

As they hurried to the Gare St. Lazare, he asked: "Will you let me see you again; or do you think you'd better not?"

She returned his long look. There was no sign of dissipation in his face, in his warm cheeks, in his erect carriage.

"I'm always fine at lunch," he added, like an invalid.

"I'm not worried," she laughed. "Take me to lunch day after tomorrow."

They hurried up the steps of the Gare St. Lazare, only to see the last carriage of the Golden Arrow disappearing toward the Channel. Julia was remorseful, because Phil had come so far.

As a sort of atonement, she went to the apartment where she lived with her aunt and tried to write a letter to him, but Dick Ragland intruded himself into her thoughts. By morning the effect of his good looks had faded a little; she was inclined to write him a note that she couldn't see him. Still, he had made her a simple appeal and she had brought it all on herself. She waited for him at half-past twelve on the appointed day.

Julia had said nothing to her aunt, who had company for luncheon and might mention his name--strange to go out with a man whose name you couldn't mention. He was late and she waited in the hall, listening to the echolalia of chatter from the luncheon party in the dining room. At one she answered the bell.

There in the outer hall stood a man whom she thought she had never seen before. His face was dead white and erratically shaven, his soft hat was crushed bunlike on his head, his shirt collar was dirty, and all except the band of his tie was out of sight. But at the moment when she recognized the figure as Dick Ragland she perceived a change which dwarfed the others into nothing; it was in his expression. His whole face was one prolonged sneer--the lids held with difficulty from covering the fixed eyes, the drooping mouth drawn up over the upper teeth, the chin wabbling like a made-over chin in which the paraffin had run--it was a face that both expressed and inspired disgust.

"H'lo," he muttered.

For a minute she drew back from him; then, at a sudden silence from the dining room that gave on the hall, inspired by the silence in the hall itself, she half pushed him over the threshold, stepped out herself and closed the door behind them.

"Oh-h-h!" she said in a single, shocked breath.

"Haven't been home since yest'day. Got involve' on a party at--"

With repugnance, she turned him around by his arm and stumbled with him down the apartment stairs, passing the concierge's wife, who peered out at them curiously from her glass room. Then they came out into the bright sunshine of the Rue Guynemer.

Against the spring freshness of the Luxembourg Gardens opposite, he was even more grotesque. He frightened her; she looked desperately up and down the street for a taxi, but one turning the corner of the Rue de Vaugirard disregarded her signal.

"Where'll we go lunch?" he asked.

"You're in no shape to go to lunch. Don't you realize? You've got to go home and sleep."

"I'm all right. I get a drink I'll be fine."

A passing cab slowed up at her gesture.

"You go home and go to sleep. You're not fit to go anywhere."

As he focused his eyes on her, realizing her suddenly as something fresh, something new and lovely, something alien to the smoky and turbulent world where he had spent his recent hours, a faint current of reason flowed through him. She saw his mouth twist with vague awe, saw him make a vague attempt to stand up straight. The taxi yawned.

"Maybe you're right. Very sorry."

"What's your address?"

He gave it and then tumbled into a corner, his face still struggling toward reality. Julia closed the door.

When the cab had driven off, she hurried across the street and into the Luxembourg Gardens as if someone were after her.

II

Quite by accident, she answered when he telephoned at seven that night. His voice was strained and shaking:

"I suppose there's not much use apologizing for this morning. I didn't know what I was doing, but that's no excuse. But if you could let me see you for a while somewhere tomorrow--just for a minute--I'd like the chance of telling you in person how terribly sorry--"

"I'm busy tomorrow."

"Well, Friday then, or any day."

"I'm sorry, I'm very busy this week."

"You mean you don't ever want to see me again?"

"Mr. Ragland, I hardly see the use of going any further with this. Really, that thing this morning was a little too much. I'm very sorry. I hope you feel better. Good-by."

She put him entirely out of her mind. She had not even associated his reputation with such a spectacle--a heavy drinker was someone who sat up late and drank champagne and maybe in the small hours rode home singing. This spectacle at high noon was something else again. Julia was through.

Meanwhile there were other men with whom she lunched at Ciro's and danced in the Bois. There was a reproachful letter from Phil Hoffman in America. She liked Phil better for having been so right about this. A fortnight passed and she would have forgotten Dick Ragland, had she not heard his name mentioned with scorn in several conversations. Evidently he had done such things before.

Then, a week before she was due to sail, she ran into him in the booking department of the White Star Line. He was as handsome--she could hardly believe her eyes. He leaned with an elbow on the desk, his fine figure erect, his yellow gloves as stainless as his clear, shining eyes. His strong, gay personality had affected the clerk who served him with fascinated deference; the stenographers behind looked up for a minute and exchanged a glance. Then he saw Julia; she nodded, and with a quick, wincing change of expression he raised his hat.

They were together by the desk a long time and the silence was oppressive.

"Isn't this a nuisance?" she said.

"Yes," he said jerkily, and then: "You going by the Olympic?"

"Oh, yes."

"I thought you might have changed."

"Of course not," she said coldly.

"I thought of changing; in fact, I was here to ask about it."

"That's absurd."

"You don't hate the sight of me? So it'll make you seasick when we pass each other on the deck?"

She smiled. He seized his advantage:

"I've improved somewhat since we last met."

"Don't talk about that."

"Well then, you have improved. You've got the loveliest costume on I ever saw."

This was presumptuous, but she felt herself shimmering a little at the compliment.

"You wouldn't consider a cup of coffee with me at the café next door, just to recover from this ordeal?"

How weak of her to talk to him like this, to let him make advances. It was like being under the fascination of a snake.

"I'm afraid I can't." Something terribly timid and vulnerable came into his face, twisting a little sinew in her heart. "Well, all right," she shocked herself by saying.

Sitting at the sidewalk table in the sunlight, there was nothing to remind her of that awful day two weeks ago. Jekyll and Hyde. He was courteous, he was charming, he was amusing. He made her feel, oh, so attractive! He presumed on nothing.

"Have you stopped drinking?" she asked.

"Not till the fifth."

"Oh!"

"Not until I said I'd stop. Then I'll stop."

When Julia rose to go, she shook her head at his suggestion of a further meeting.

"I'll see you on the boat. After your twenty-eighth birthday."

"All right; one more thing: It fits in with the high price of crime that I did something inexcusable to the one girl I've ever been in love with in my life."

She saw him the first day on board, and then her heart sank into her shoes as she realized at last how much she wanted him. No matter what his past was, no matter what he had done. Which was not to say that she would ever let him know, but only that he moved her chemically more than anyone she had ever met, that all other men seemed pale beside him.

He was popular on the boat; she heard that he was giving a party on the night of his twenty-eighth birthday. Julia was not invited; when they met they spoke pleasantly, nothing more.

It was the day after the fifth that she found him stretched in his deck chair looking wan and white. There were wrinkles on his fine brow and around his eyes, and his hand, as he reached out for a cup of bouillon, was trembling. He was still there in the late afternoon, visibly suffering, visibly miserable. After three times around, Julia was irresistibly impelled to speak to him:

"Has the new era begun?"

He made a feeble effort to rise, but she motioned him not to and sat on the next chair.

"You look tired."

"I'm just a little nervous. This is the first day in five years that I haven't had a drink."

"It'll be better soon."

"I know," he said grimly.

"Don't weaken."

"I won't."

"Can't I help you in any way? Would you like a bromide?"

"I can't stand bromides," he said almost crossly. "No, thanks, I mean."

Julia stood up: "I know you feel better alone. Things will be brighter tomorrow."

"Don't go, if you can stand me."

Julia sat down again.

"Sing me a song--can you sing?"

"What kind of a song?"

"Something sad--some sort of blues."

She sang him Libby Holman's "This is how the story ends," in a low, soft voice.

"That's good. Now sing another. Or sing that again."

"All right. If you like, I'll sing to you all afternoon."

III

The second day in New York he called her on the phone. "I've missed you so," he said. "Have you missed me?"

"I'm afraid I have," she said reluctantly.

"Much?"

"I've missed you a lot. Are you better?"

"I'm all right now. I'm still just a little nervous, but I'm starting work tomorrow. When can I see you?"

"When you want."

"This evening then. And look--say that again."

"What?"

"That you're afraid you have missed me."

"I'm afraid that I have," Julia said obediently.

"Missed me," he added.

"I'm afraid I have missed you."

"All right. It sounds like a song when you say it."

"Good-by, Dick."

"Good-by, Julia dear."

She stayed in New York two months instead of the fortnight she had intended, because he would not let her go. Work took the place of drink in the daytime, but afterward he must see Julia.

Sometimes she was jealous of his work when he telephoned that he was too tired to go out after the theater. Lacking drink, night life was less than nothing to him--something quite spoiled and well lost. For Julia, who never drank, it was a stimulus in itself--the music and the parade of dresses and the handsome couple they made dancing together. At first they saw Phil Hoffman once in a while; Julia considered that he took the matter rather badly; then they didn't see him any more.

A few unpleasant incidents occurred. An old schoolmate, Esther Cary, came to her to ask if she knew of Dick Ragland's reputation. Instead of growing angry, Julia invited her to meet Dick and was delighted with the ease with which Esther's convictions were changed. There were other, small, annoying episodes, but Dick's misdemeanors had, fortunately, been confined to Paris and assumed here a far-away unreality. They loved each other deeply now--the memory of that morning slowly being effaced from Julia's imagination--but she wanted to be sure.

"After six months, if everything goes along like this, we'll announce our engagement. After another six months we'll be married."

"Such a long time," he mourned.

"But there were five years before that," Julia answered. "I trust you with my heart and with my mind, but something else says wait. Remember, I'm also deciding for my children."

Those five years--oh, so lost and gone.

In August, Julia went to California for two months to see her family. She wanted to know how Dick would get along alone. They wrote every day; his letters were by turns cheerful, depressed, weary and hopeful. His work was going better. As things came back to him, his uncle had begun really to believe in him, but all the time he missed his Julia so. It was when an occasional note of despair began to appear that she cut her visit short by a week and came East to New York.

"Oh, thank God you're here!" he cried as they linked arms and walked out of the Grand Central station. "It's been so hard. Half a dozen times lately I've wanted to go on a bust and I had to think of you, and you were so far away."

"Darling--darling, you're so tired and pale. You're working too hard."

"No, only that life is so bleak alone. When I go to bed my mind churns on and on. Can't we get married sooner?"

"I don't know; we'll see. You've got your Julia near you now, and nothing matters."

After a week, Dick's depression lifted. When he was sad, Julia made him her baby, holding his handsome head against her breast, but she liked it best when he was confident and could cheer her up, making her laugh and feel taken care of and secure. She had rented an apartment with another girl and she took courses in biology and domestic science in Columbia. When deep fall came, they went to football games and the new shows together, and walked through the first snow in Central Park, and several times a week spent long evenings together in front of her fire. But time was going by and they were both impatient. Just before Christmas, an unfamiliar visitor--Phil Hoffman--presented himself at her door. It was the first time in many months. New York, with its quality of many independent ladders set side by side, is unkind to even the meetings of close friends; so, in the case of strained relations, meetings are easy to avoid.

And they were strange to each other. Since his expressed skepticism of Dick, he was automatically her enemy; on another count, she saw that he had improved, some of the hard angles were worn off; he was now an assistant district attorney, moving around with increasing confidence through his profession.

"So you're going to marry Dick?" he said. "When?"

"Soon now. When mother comes East."

He shook his head emphatically. "Julia, don't marry Dick. This isn't jealousy--I know when I am licked--but it seems awful for a lovely girl like you to take a blind dive into a lake full of rocks. What makes you think that people change their courses? Sometimes they dry up or even flow into a parallel channel, but I've never known anybody to change."

"Dick's changed."

"Maybe so. But isn't that an enormous 'maybe'? If he was unattractive and you liked him, I'd say go ahead with it. Maybe I'm all wrong, but it's so darn obvious that what fascinates you is that handsome pan of his and those attractive manners."

"You don't know him," Julia answered loyally. "He's different with me. You don't know how gentle he is, and responsive. Aren't you being rather small and mean?"

"Hm." Phil thought for a moment. "I want to see you again in a few days. Or perhaps I'll speak to Dick."

"You let Dick alone," she cried. "He has enough to worry him without your nagging him. If you were his friend you'd try to help him instead of coming to me behind his back."

"I'm your friend first."

"Dick and I are one person now."

But three days later Dick came to see her at an hour when he would usually have been at the office.

"I'm here under compulsion," he said lightly, "under threat of exposure by Phil Hoffman."

Her heart dropping like a plummet. "Has he given up?" she thought. "Is he drinking again?"

"It's about a girl. You introduced me to her last summer and told me to be very nice to her--Esther Cary."

Now her heart was beating slowly.

"After you went to California I was lonesome and I ran into her. She'd liked me that day, and for a while we saw quite a bit of each other. Then you came back and I broke it off. It was a little difficult; I hadn't realized that she was so interested."

"I see." Her voice was starved and aghast.

"Try and understand. Those terribly lonely evenings. I think if it hadn't been for Esther, I'd have fallen off the wagon. I never loved her--I never loved anybody but you--but I had to see somebody who liked me."

He put his arm around her, but she felt cold all over and he drew away.

"Then any woman would have done," Julia said slowly. "It didn't matter who."

"No!" he cried.

"I stayed away so long to let you stand on your own feet and get back your self-respect by yourself."

"I only love you, Julia."

"But any woman can help you. So you don't really need me, do you?"

His face wore that vulnerable look that Julia had seen several times before; she sat on the arm of his chair and ran her hand over his cheek.

"Then what do you bring me?" she demanded. "I thought that there'd be the accumulated strength of having beaten your weakness. What do you bring me now?"

"Everything I have."

She shook her head. "Nothing. Just your good looks--and the head waiter at dinner last night had that."

They talked for two days and decided nothing. Sometimes she would pull him close and reach up to his lips that she loved so well, but her arms seemed to close around straw.

"I'll go away and give you a chance to think it over," he said despairingly. "I can't see any way of living without you, but I suppose you can't marry a man you don't trust or believe in. My uncle wanted me to go to London on some business--"

The night he left, it was sad on the dim pier. All that kept her from breaking was that it was not an image of strength that was leaving her; she would be just as strong without him. Yet as the murky lights fell on the fine structure of his brow and chin, as she saw the faces turn toward him, the eyes that followed him, an awful emptiness seized her and she wanted to say: "Never mind, dear; we'll try it together."

But try what? It was human to risk the toss between failure and success, but to risk the desperate gamble between adequacy and disaster--

"Oh, Dick, be good and be strong and come back to me. Change, change, Dick--change!"

"Good-by, Julia--good-by."

She last saw him on the deck, his profile cut sharp as a cameo against a match as he lit a cigarette.

IV

It was Phil Hoffman who was to be with her at the beginning and the end. It was he who broke the news as gently as it could be broken. He reached her apartment at half-past eight and carefully threw away the morning paper outside. Dick Ragland had disappeared at sea.

After her first wild burst of grief, he became purposely a little cruel.

"He knew himself. His will had given out; he didn't want life any more. And, Julia, just to show you how little you can possibly blame yourself, I'll tell you this: He'd hardly gone to his office for four months--since you went to California. He wasn't fired because of his uncle; the business he went to London on was of no importance at all. After his first enthusiasm was gone he'd given up."

She looked at him sharply. "He didn't drink, did he? He wasn't drinking?"

For a fraction of a second Phil hesitated. "No, he didn't drink; he kept his promise--he held on to that."

"That was it," she said. "He kept his promise and he killed himself doing it."

Phil waited uncomfortably.

"He did what he said he would and broke his heart doing it," she went on chokingly. "Oh, isn't life cruel sometimes--so cruel, never to let anybody off. He was so brave--he died doing what he said he'd do."

Phil was glad he had thrown away the newspaper that hinted of Dick's gay evening in the bar--one of many gay evenings that Phil had known of in the past few months. He was relieved that was over, because Dick's weakness had threatened the happiness of the girl he loved; but he was terribly sorry for him--even understanding how it was necessary for him to turn his maladjustment to life toward one mischief or another--but he was wise enough to leave Julia with the dream that she had saved out of wreckage.

There was a bad moment a year later, just before their marriage, when she said:

"You'll understand the feeling I have and always will have about Dick, won't you, Phil? It wasn't just his good looks. I believed in him--and I was right in a way. He broke rather than bent; he was a ruined man, but not a bad man. In my heart I knew when I first looked at him."

Phil winced, but he said nothing. Perhaps there was more behind it than they knew. Better let it all alone in the depths of her heart and the depths of the sea.

Lector House believes that a society develops through a two-fold approach of continuous learning and adaptation, which is derived from the study of classic literary works spread across the historic timeline of literature records. Therefore, we aim at reviving, repairing and redeveloping all those inaccessible or damaged but historically as well as culturally important literature across subjects so that the future generations may have an opportunity to study and learn from past works to embark upon a journey of creating a better future.

This book is a result of an effort made by Lector House towards making a contribution to the preservation and repair of original ancient works which might hold historical significance to the approach of continuous learning across subjects.

HAPPY READING & LEARNING!

LECTOR HOUSE LLP
E-MAIL: lectorpublishing@gmail.com

9 789353 420598

Printed in the USA
CPSIA information can be obtained
at www.ICGtesting.com
LVHW091334311223
767834LV00047B/618

